story
ZAI WHITAKER

Salim Mamoo and Me

pictures
PRABHA MALLYA

I was about six years old, and a bit confused. I had a famous uncle. My friends, and cousins, and teachers – my whole world – said, “Wow WOW, how lucky you are to have such a famous uncle!” And I’d smile and try to look lucky. But I had a smile outside and a frown inside.

Because I had a problem. And not a small one either.

Salim mamoo was a bird expert. This kind of expert is called an ornithologist. He had written so many books on birds that I thought his pen would run out of ink.

He was a superstar in the world of animals and birds. He was friends with kings and queens and many Important People. Nehru and Indira Gandhi. And he went to London and Germany and all those kinds of places. He knew big-big people and went to big-big places, said everyone.

He walked thousands of miles every year, in forests and on beaches and on mountains and in valleys, studying birds. He would look at them for hours, and sometimes shoot one to find out who it actually was.

"Thank goodness they don't need to do this to people," I said to my sister.

So what was my problem? Having a famous bird uncle should be fun, right? Well, it wasn't. It was the opposite of fun. Total un-fun.

My problem was that it wasn't just Salim mamoo who was a bird star. My whole family were bird experts. My father and mother and brother and sister and our cook Paul. They flipped pages of Salim mamoo's bird book and found the bird they'd seen in the garden, or park, or forest, or on a trip somewhere.

"Ah!" they'd shout in delight. "Orange-headed ground thrush!"

And I felt left out.

I wanted to be like them. I wanted to recognise the song of the oriole, and the fork tail of the drongo, and the difference between the male and female paradise flycatcher. But I wanted to become an expert without paying attention, because school took away all the attention that I had. I didn't have any left for other things.

This made me so sad.
But I couldn't talk about it.
Years passed. I grew taller
and taller and so did my
problem. The worst part
was I began to hate birds.

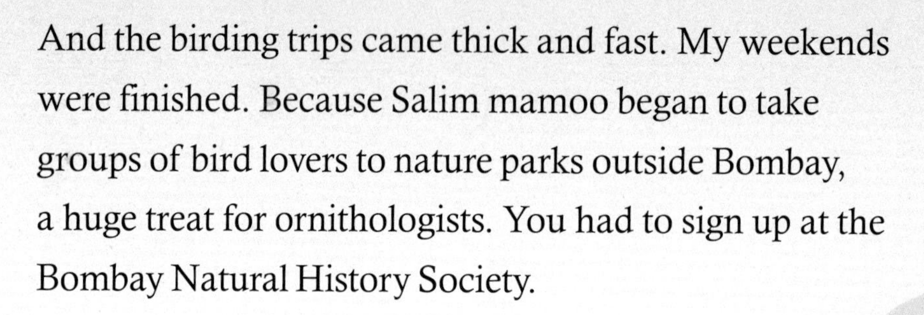

And the birding trips came thick and fast. My weekends were finished. Because Salim mamoo began to take groups of bird lovers to nature parks outside Bombay, a huge treat for ornithologists. You had to sign up at the Bombay Natural History Society.

I think my father must have signed up for all of us, for our whole lives. From then on, my only Sunday memory is being woken up at five – it felt like midnight – and being told to hurry up and wash, hurry up and brush, hurry up and dress, hurry up and go to the car.

Salim mamoo's large blue Willys jeep would be lurking at the junction, filled with the Bandra Birders.

Other birders would arrive from different parts of the city… All looking excited and determined to come first, which meant having the longest bird list! We were the Andheri Birders. The Dadar Birders never brought a proper picnic, but just ate whatever the rest of us offered them. When Paul prepared our picnic he'd put in some plain bread-jam sandwiches and wink at me. "Give to Dadar people," he'd say.

When a birder asked me "What's that?" I didn't want to say, "I don't know." No one likes to say they don't know. So I thought up a good plan. And it worked really well. I pretended I hadn't seen the bird at all. "Where? Where?" I'd say, even if it was a huge bird like a peacock and it was sitting a foot away from my nose.

It worked really, really well. For a while. Then, one day, Salim mamoo saw me in action and got worried. He spoke to my mother. “She didn’t see the pipit that was sitting right in front of us! She may need glasses.”

And so my pet name at school changed to Owlet. I had the most ugly pair of spectacles in class. "She doesn't need glasses," the eye-doctor kept saying to my mother. "Of course she does. What do you know?" We always knew best.

Wearing the largest glasses in Bombay, I no longer had an excuse. The next bird watching trip was coming up, closer and closer.

I had a sleepless night. I imagined every kind of possibility. In one series of snapshots, a flock of huge, obvious, common birds landed right in front of me and I didn't know what they were. Everyone's faces were embarrassed, from forehead to chin. Even their noses. I got out of bed to shake off the fears. I began dressing in the inky darkness. I was ready by five.

Soon there was a bustle in the kitchen. "Wonderful, wonderful," I heard my mother murmur to my father. "I knew she'd become interested. Imagine! Up and ready so early! Makes me so happy."

Hmmm, I thought. And off we went, the others sharing lists of must-sees and might-sees and I mentally listing hope-not-to-sees, such as bay-backed shrikes because I always thought they were tree-pies.

My mother took my glasses so she could clean them for me with her sari pallu. Ouch.

Perhaps I should go lame today, I decided, and sit on the culvert and writhe in pain, and miss the entire thing. But that meant missing the sandwiches too. If you were in pain, I mean properly, you couldn't show too much interest in food.

But God looked after me that day. I didn't have to do a thing. When we got to the forest trail an hour later and the what's-that, what's-this started, and I began to say where-where, my mother looked at me in sympathy and cried, "Oh, I forgot your glasses in the car! I cleaned them… and left them on the seat! How silly of me. Poor Zai!"

Poor Zai was delighted. The problem had been solved. Salim mamoo even held my hand so I wouldn't trip and fall over fallen deadwood and roots.

And soon after that, everything changed. I told Amma my eyes were fine, but not my brain. I told them my bird-names problem.

"I can't believe this!" my sister said. "So what if you're not interested? It just doesn't matter!"

"Of course it doesn't!" said my father.

"Poor old Zai," said my brother. "You've been miserable for nothing. Here, have a treat." And he whacked me with his cricket bat. "I'll love you even if you can't tell a cormorant from a darter."

I still remember the lightness of that day. And then a funny thing happened. I began to love those bird mornings. It dawned on me that you could love birds without knowing their names. I began to love their colours and crests and wattles and plumes and all the other extras. They were pretty stylish.

And then, when I was about six inches taller, but still short for my age, something amazing happened. We were on a high cliff. The Andheri, Bandra and Dadar birders were watching a pair of soaring raptors in the sky below us. “Shikra!” shouted Andheri. “Eh, fool. Harriers,” said Bandra, with an insulting gesture. Dadar shouted some other ignorant name and got laughed at by both Andheri and Bandra. Salim mamoo was on his way up. He would know for sure.

I had been watching the way the wings dipped and turned, dipped and turned. "Isn't it… isn't it… could it be… the black-winged kite?" I said hesitantly.

"It is," said a croaky voice from behind me and Salim mamoo's rough hand landed on my back. I squinted into the distance, trying not to look victorious.

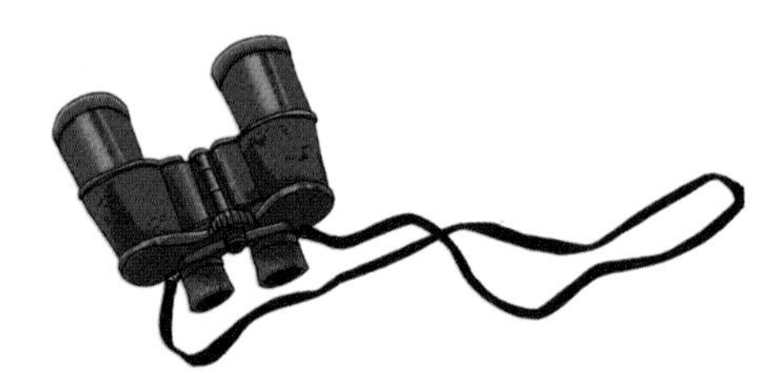

Salim Mamoo and Me

ISBN 978-93-5046-927-9

First published in India, 2017

Published by
Tulika Publishers, 24/1 Ganapathy Colony Third Street, Teynampet,
Chennai 600 018, India
email tulikabooks@vsnl.com *website* www.tulikabooks.com

Printed and bound by
Sudarsan Graphics, 27 Neelakanta Mehta Street, T. Nagar,
Chennai 600 017, India